The Princess and the Dragon

MiLeS KeLLY

There once lived a young princess called Charlotte.

Princess Charlotte preferred being called Charlie. She looked like a princess, but she **didn't behave like one!**

Charlie didn't like dresses or dancing, and she didn't want to ever marry a prince.

Charlie's father, the king, was hoping to find a new queen, so there were often **royal parties** at the palace.

"Do try to behave like a **proper princess, Charlotte!**" the king would say before each party.

But Charlie didn't like wearing ribbons and smart shoes, and looking pretty all the time.

Other royal young ladies
liked to wander through
the palace gardens and sit
under the trees.

Charlie preferred **climbing the trees** and hanging about in them.

Every day the king said the same thing: "Please try to behave like a **proper princess**, Charlotte!" But Charlie was happy just the way she was.

To the king's dismay, Charlie's **best** friend was a dragon called Dylan.

They played rough and tumble muddy games, so everyone stayed away from them.

But Charlie and Dylan **always had fun** together and understood each other perfectly.

One day, Charlie and Dylan were **playing** in the woods.

They were **hanging upside down** in their favourite tree, when they heard someone nearby.

It was a witch!
And she was **chanting** to herself.

"Turn the palace into sand,
So I may finally **rule this land**,
Send me water, so the king may fall,
With this curse I will have it all!"

Charlie and Dylan didn't dare move as an **explosion of light** shot towards the palace.

The witch **cackled happily** to herself. "Once the moon begins to shine, This kingdom will be mine, mine, MINE!"

As soon as the witch left, Charlie and Dylan flew home.

"We've got to **warn everyone**," said Charlie as they flew. "We haven't got long before the sun sets!"

But the king was furious that Charlie was late home.

He sent her straight to her room and **locked the door**, without letting Charlie talk at all!

Quickly Charlie whistled to Dylan and together they **came** up with a plan to save everyone.

Charlie and Dylan flew from her bedroom and swooped across the palace courtyard.

They scooped up mud from the lake and threw it at everyone!

"That got everyone's attention!" said Charlie, as they watched people running for the gates.

"Charlotte!" yelled the king. "Why can't you behave like a proper princess!"

"A witch has put a spell on the palace," shouted Charlie.

"The lake water is rising. Everyone needs to get to higher ground!"

"Dylan!" said Charlie. "Take the children up to the hill. I'll help everyone here."

While Dylan flew away with the smallest children,
Charlie helped her father climb the flagpole.

The guards **threw ropes** up into the trees so everyone could climb higher than the water.

It didn't look as if there was anything Charlie could do to **save the palace** though.

As the spell **worked its magic**, the entire palace turned to sand, and the lake water rushed in.

Suddenly, there was an ear-piercing screech and Dylan swooped down, roaring **huge jets of fire**.

The witch shrieked as **whirls of sand** were whisked up by the hot wind.

In an instant, the whole building became a beautiful, glittering glass palace and the **witch vanished!**

"You **saved us all**," said the king as he came down from the flagpole.

"For once Charlie, I'm happy you didn't behave like a **proper princess!**"